PANTHERA
tigris

WRITTEN BY
Sylvain Alzial

ILLUSTRATED BY
Hélène Rajcak

TRANSLATED FROM THE FRENCH BY
Vineet Lal AND **Sarah Ardizzone**

EERDMANS BOOKS FOR YOUNG READERS

GRAND RAPIDS, MICHIGAN

1. SCHOLAR'S BRAIN	2. MEMORY ZONE	3. SPEED READING ZONE
4. LEARNING ZONE	5. KNOWLEDGE REPOSITORY	6. BUTTON FOR RECITING

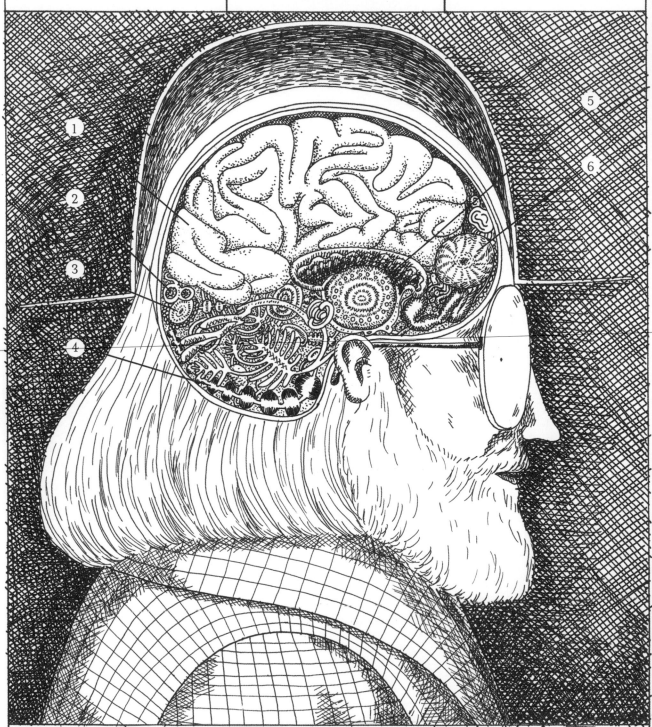

PLATE 1. INSIDE THE SCHOLAR'S HEAD

There was once a man who knew a great deal.
He was a small gentleman with a black hat and a white beard,
and he always carried a thick book filled with everything he knew.
This scholar would spend his days reading, and his knowledge
was astounding. He knew the history of the WORLD, the history
of the SKY and EARTH, the history of MEN and WOMEN,
the history of ANIMALS, the history of INSECTS, the history
of CITIES, the history of SCIENCE, the history of the PAST
and the FUTURE . . .

His head was stuffed with all manner of learned things.

One day, while consulting an encyclopedia in the library, he realized he knew nothing about Bengal tigers! Enraged by this gap in his knowledge, he frantically buried himself in all the books he could find about these big cats.

Following many long months of research, he decided to set off for the Indian jungle in search of the famous tiger.

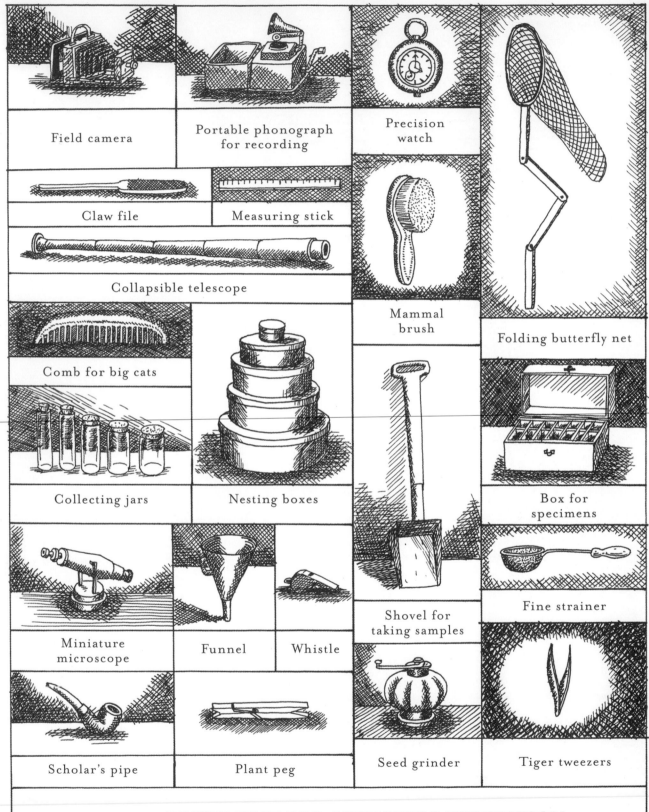

Field camera

Portable phonograph for recording

Precision watch

Claw file

Measuring stick

Collapsible telescope

Mammal brush

Folding butterfly net

Comb for big cats

Collecting jars

Nesting boxes

Box for specimens

Miniature microscope

Funnel

Whistle

Shovel for taking samples

Fine strainer

Scholar's pipe

Plant peg

Seed grinder

Tiger tweezers

PLATE 2 . EQUIPMENT FOR SCIENTIFIC EXPEDITION

After a very long journey, the scholar finally arrived and asked a local hunter to guide him through the jungle. The hunter was a rather simple young man who had never read a book in his life, nor set foot inside a school. But he had been exploring the wild Indian forest ever since he was a child, and knew it like the back of his hand.

TIGER . PANTHERA TIGRIS

SNOW LEOPARD
PANTHERA UNCIA

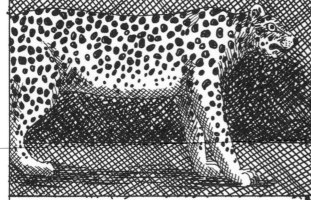

LEOPARD . PANTHERA PARDUS

LION . PANTHERA LEO

JAGUAR . PANTHERA ONCA

PLATE 3 . BIG CATS OF THE GENUS "PANTHERA"

When he was introduced to the scholar, the young man
was a little awestruck, and all he could say was:

"Good day, Sir. You see, the tigers in this forest are . . . "

"Now then, young man," interjected the scholar, "did you
know that, according to the Linnaean classification of 1758,
the Bengal tiger is called *Panthera tigris tigris*? Did you know
that it belongs to the order Carnivora, the family Felidae,
the sub-family Pantherinae, and the genus *Panthera*? And
did you also know that the Bengal tiger lives principally in
tropical forests, jungles, and swampy regions, and that it
urinates to mark its territory?"

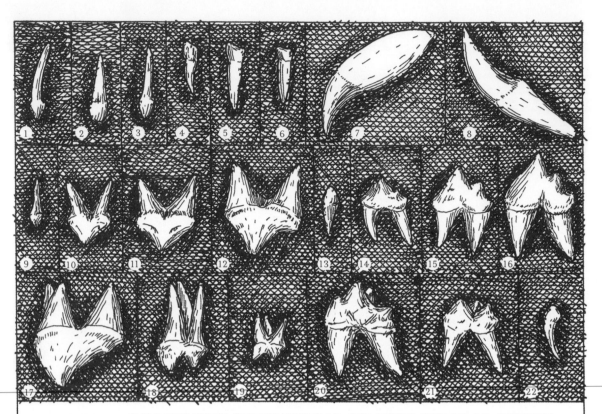

FIGURE 1 . COMPLETE DENTITION OF THE BENGAL TIGER
1 to 6 : incisors / 7 and 8 : canines / 9 to 16 : premolars / 17 to 22 : molars

Armed with this first lesson, they entered the forest under a blazing sun. For several days, the young guide led the great scholar through the dense, ominous jungle. He tried again and again to offer a warning:

"Sir, you see, the tigers in this forest are . . . "

But the scholar kept going without letting him finish his sentence: "Did you know that *Panthera tigris* possesses highly developed carnivorous teeth, notably the fourth upper premolar and the first lower molar?"

"Did you know that male tigers weigh between 400 and 550 pounds, and females between 220 and 350 pounds? Did you also know that tigers have formidable retractable claws four inches long? Or that this animal is able to change its position, depending on the wind, in order to mask its own scent?"

The scientific expedition continued like this for many days, to the drone of the great scholar's endless monologue.

One morning, the young guide spotted claw marks at the foot of a tree. He turned to the scholar, his voice filled with concern:

"Sir, you see, the tigers in this forest are . . . "

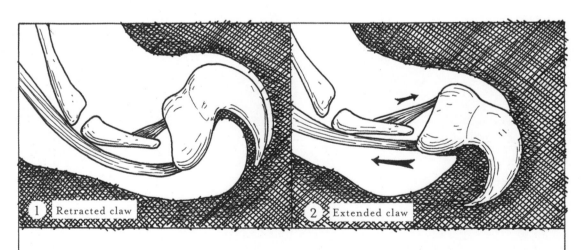

FIGURE 2 . DIAGRAM OF THE TIGER'S RETRACTABLE CLAWS

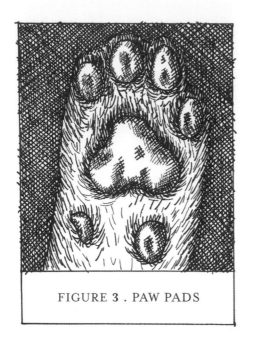

FIGURE **3** . PAW PADS

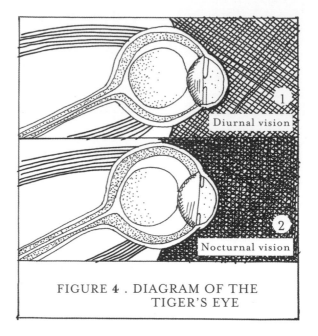

Diurnal vision

Nocturnal vision

FIGURE **4** . DIAGRAM OF THE
TIGER'S EYE

"In fact," interrupted the scholar, "did you know that the
pads on a tiger's paws are made of an elastic membrane,
allowing this noble beast to move around in complete silence?
Or that its diet, in calorific terms, is equal to $y = 1.97 + 0.034 \times 2$?
And that's not all: did you know that the tiger has excellent
eyesight, and that its whiskers are called vibrissae?"

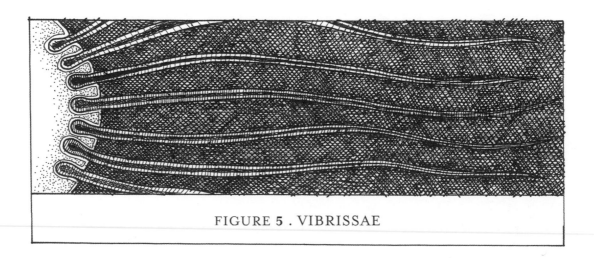

FIGURE **5** . VIBRISSAE

All of a sudden, as they were passing through a shady clearing . . .
they finally came upon . . . A TIGER!
The animal was perfectly still, magnificent, with ferocious eyes,
flaming fur, and claws as sharp as razor blades.

At the sight of the creature, the young hunter
instinctively climbed up a tree, out of harm's way.

As for the great scholar, he tried desperately
to put a brave face on things.

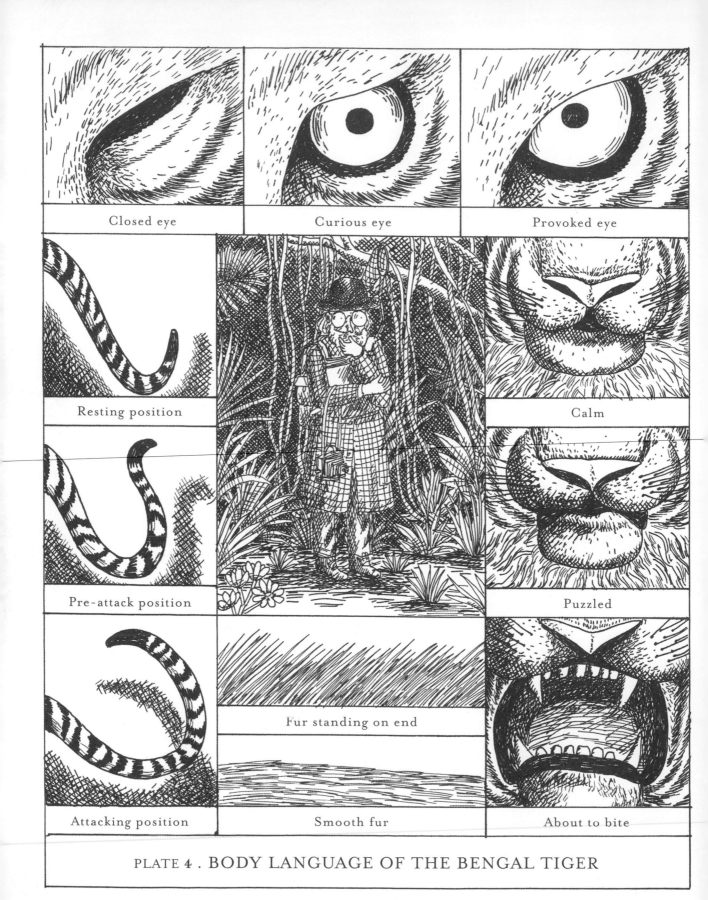

Closed eye

Curious eye

Provoked eye

Resting position

Calm

Pre-attack position

Puzzled

Attacking position

Fur standing on end

Smooth fur

About to bite

PLATE 4 . BODY LANGUAGE OF THE BENGAL TIGER

Of course he knew every species of tiger, as well as every
meaning of the word TIGER. He could quote the precise
number of teeth in its jaws and hairs on its body.
But what should he do when this wild beast was breathing
before his very eyes?

PLATE **5** . ATTEMPT AT DIALOGUE WITH THE TIGER

Taken aback, he flicked nervously through his thick book,
searching for how to say "GOOD DAY" in tiger language,
and mumbled "WAOUH?"
But the beast didn't seem to understand at all.
The scholar racked his brains to recall the tigerish expressions
he'd seen in zoological anthologies, and tried his luck with:

"GRR" in a rather feeble voice...
as well as "RRRRAAHHH"...

and even "PFFF"...

The tiger, who couldn't understand a word of what the human was saying, was now

VERY ANGRY INDEED.

It came closer, and closer . . . and let out a terrible

ROOOAAARR

that boomed far and wide across the forest.

Horrified, the scholar dropped his book and fled without further ado, screaming in terror.

Once the tiger was far enough away,
the young man came down from his tree.
He picked up the book, which now had two enormous holes in it,
and finished his sentence at last:

"You see, Sir,
the tigers in this forest are

DAN-GER-OUS!"